Mexi's Christmas Tale

By
Maxine k Brown

This book is the third in "The adventures of Mexi, the boat dog". Christmas is a time to be with friends, family and loved ones. It is essential that everyone feels special throughout life and especially around Christmas. Mexi

I ran into my mum and dad's bedroom and said, "quick, you've got to wake up" my dad shot up and said what is the matter, Mexi? Mum panicked and jumped out of bed and nearly trod on me. I said it was December the first. This means two things. Today I can open my advent calendar, and also, Father Christmas is coming in a few weeks. Mum said I needed to go back to my bed and calm down, as Father Christmas would be watching me, and he likes little ones to be good and listen to their elders. I bowed my head and said OK, but can we please get up soon? We have lots to do. Dad said I had to stay in bed until half past seven, which meant I still had one hour to wait.

I went back to my bed under the dinette. This is under the table in the middle of the boat. It would be under your dining table if you lived in a house.

Just after half past seven, mum said we had to go for a walk first as I needed a wee. She said dad would get breakfast ready, and then I could open my first day of the advent calendar after I had eaten all of my breakfast. I said OK. I wasn't very happy as I really wanted to open the advent calendar, but I knew that I must be good; otherwise, Father Christmas would be sad, and I may not even get any presents on Christmas morning.

We went for our morning walk, it was freezing, and when you walked on the grass, it made a crackly noise because it was frozen. It was white all over, and I loved running and biting the grass; it was like having lots of little ice cubes in my mouth. I saw Amanda, who was taking Nyx for her morning walk. I shouted to Nyx, are you excited it's December? Nyx was a bit confused as this was her first Christmas, so she wasn't sure what was happening. She ran up to me and said that Wayne was getting her breakfast ready, and he had said that after she had eaten all of it up, there was a thing called an advent calendar that she could open. I said that was great and explained that for the next twenty-five days each morning, she could open the advent calendar, and there would be a treat inside it. I did tell her too that she must be good because last year when I was naughty one day my mum wouldn't let me open it and she opened it and gave the treat to the ducks. Nyx said thank you for the warning, and we had a run around while Amanda and mum had a chat. I did hear them mention Christmas decorations and something called a marquee. I later found out this was a huge tent, and we would have a party there.

We all went back to our narrowboats to have breakfast. Usually, we travel around, stopping on different canals, but my mum and dad had decided we would stay in Brinklow marina, known as the marina of dreams. They thought it would be great fun as friends would also be there, and we could take trips out when the weather was good.

After breakfast, mum said we would all help decorate the marquee with a Christmas tree and decorations. Dad said he was coming; I was told I had to be good and listen to them at all times. I did struggle to do this, which used to get me into trouble so often, but I said I would try my hardest.
We went over to the marquee, and dad pulled our trolly, which was full of brightly coloured tinsel and lots of lights and hanging sparkly things, plus a huge angel for the top of the tree.

There were lots of others at the marquee. They had Christmas songs blaring out of the speakers, which was great. I quickly saw Nyx, who was playing with Max and Digby. These were her friends who lived on a narrowboat with their cat, Marmite, and their mum and dad, Claire and Matt. I showed them all the decorations we had brought, and they said they had loads too.
I pulled a very long piece of sparkly tinsel out of the trolly, Nyx grabbed the other end, and we started

running around, and we wrapped Digby and Max in the tinsel, and they started to giggle. My mum shouted me over to her. She then said to behave and passed me lots of Christmas decorations to decorate the marquee.
After all the little bits had been put up, it was time for the dads to bring in the enormous Christmas tree. WOW, it was sooo very high. It nearly touched the top of the marquee.
The four of us stood and looked up at the tree as the parents and their friends decorated it. We were told to go and play for a while as they thought we might get in the way. We didn't mind. We decided to go and dance and sing Christmas songs and also started chatting with each other about Christmas and what we thought would happen on Christmas morning. Nyx and Digby were very excited because this was their first Christmas. There were only a few final touches for the tree, to place the huge angel on top of the tree and switch on the twinkling lights.

We decided that Nyx and Digby should do those jobs as they were the youngest and had never done that before. We counted down five, four, three, two, one and pow. The tree lit up brightly, and the angel looked beautiful on top of the tree. We all clapped and then said goodnight, as it had been a very long day, and we needed to have our tea and get ready for bed.

My dad put me to bed after I had tea and washed and cleaned my teeth. He read me a Christmas story which was so lovely, and I quickly fell asleep and I dreamt of snow, reindeer and Father Christmas.

I woke up early but remembered to stay on my bed and play for a bit until mum or dad said I could get up. I started to draw a picture. It was my perfect Christmas party; it had all my doggy friends and little human friends, plus the llamas I had met when we cruised earlier in the year. I also thought I would have the moorhens at the Christmas party as they were my friends now. I had learnt that I must be kind to everyone and, of course, goosey and the ducks.

Dad shouted Mexi, at eight o clock. He said what are you up to? Are you not coming for a walk and to eat breakfast?
I showed dad my picture, and he could see what I had been doing and asked, " Is this what you would like? A fun Christmas party.

I quickly said this would be perfect. It would be such fun to see all my friends together. He said we would have to see as it would take a lot to organise. I understood and quickly asked if I could open my advent calendar. He said I could but must eat all my breakfast first. I shrugged and said OKAY.

After breakfast, I went to call for Nyx. It was lovely at the marina as it was safe for us to play. We had a very big field on which we could play ball. We had to stay away from the pond and the little road that went around it, though. I was telling Nyx all about the picture I had drawn she sounded excited about it too. We said wouldn’t it be fun if we could have a party like that.

After playing for a little while, Digby and Max came and played too. We ran around lots and lots and tired ourselves out. The marina had started to put up more lights, and it was beginning to look very Christmassy.

The next few days flew by so fast. Each morning though, I opened my advent calendar and enjoyed my treat almost daily. I say almost because my mum didn't let me have the treat twice and gave it to the ducks. I suppose she was right. On one occasion, I didn't eat my breakfast; the other one was when I was very cheeky and didn't want to listen to her when she shouted for me to come back. She had given me a couple of chances too. Sometimes it's so difficult to be good all the time.

I was called into the galley (this is the kitchen on a boat) early one morning. I panicked, trying to think what I had done, but really this time, I hadn't. I had been good since mum told me off a week ago. Mum and dad were waiting for me. What did they want? I thought, hi, are you both ok? They replied yes, we have something to tell you. Oh, that's okay. I thought I was in trouble. We've been chatting with your friend's mums and dads, and we have decided to turn the picture you drew into real life.

I said what do you mean we are going to have a Christmas party, and all my friends are coming? They both said yes together. What, even my little human friends too, and the llamas? They said yes. Wow, I ran around wagging my tail so hard it knocked the books off the shelves. Whoops.

I ran around to Wayne and Amanda's boat to tell Nyx. She was also very excited as her mum and dad had just told her. We flew down to see the others and tell them it was quickly going around the marina, and the ducks even heard us and promptly told goosey and the moorhens.

The planning had started for the Christmas Tale party. Mum had emailed my human friends to let them know when and where the party would be. It was happening on the 23rd of December, two days before Christmas day. This allows the people not living at the marina to get back.

I asked the ducks to fly to the Grand Union Canal near Foxton to let Lucy, Larry, Louise and Logan llama know about the party and to say they could stay for the night in the field on the marina. I also said if they saw goosey or the moorhens on the way to let them know, there would be plenty of room in the pond on the big field for the night for them to stay.

We heard back from Gary and Nikki; they would come with their new puppy Dixie. Along with Dale Primrose and two of my favourite little humans, Lily and Noah. I don't think I can wait another ten days. I'm so excited now.

I was so pleased the days were short because they passed by quickly. Wayne was getting all the music sorted out. He had said he would put lots of lovely

Christmas songs on the list and some silly songs that everyone could dance to. I asked him to put the Baby Shark song on as a surprise for my dad. I couldn't wait to see his face. (He really didn't like this song ?)
Amanda was helping my mum make tasty treats. And cakes.
They were making lots of different ones so that there were some for us all. It took some planning, but they were very organised. I was even allowed to help a bit and make the Christmas cookies. We had doggie ones in the shape of a bone, and they had green peanut butter on the ends, so they looked a bit like a cracker.

My human granny and granddad were coming too and bringing my best friend, Canna. They were giving Charlie a lift down. He was Sebina's dog, and I loved playing with him. He likes my favourite game too, which is chase.

Nyx and I started to think of games we could play. I said what about musical cushions. This was an alternative to musical chairs. All the dogs could sit on a cushion, which would be fun. We could play sleeping statues, too; this

is where the music plays, and when it stops, you have to stand still until the music starts again. I might find this very difficult as I like to move around a lot.
We asked mum if we could have a little pond so the ducks could play a game. They would have to pick out floating Christmas baubles for a prize. The llamas could play the other games with us as they could lay down near the cushions and stand still for the statue game.

It was all coming together, but we still had a few days until everyone arrived. Mum suggested that I write out my Christmas letter to Father Christmas. She said that it would be nice too to write a list of Christmas gifts for all my friends that I could give them. Then once this was done, we could go to the pet shop and buy the gifts and wrap them in nice Christmas paper. I was allowed to help, mum said, as long as I didn't mess about.
We headed off to the pet supermarket. I loved going there; I could see the rabbits and guinea pigs, I loved the little furry animals, and they always came to the front of their cages to say hello.

We managed to get all of the little pressies for everyone, and when we got home, mum got the Sellotape and paper out so we could wrap everything up. The Sellotape was not easy to use, I kept getting it stuck to my paws and fur, but eventually, we got everything wrapped and put in a big sack ready for the Christmas party. We wanted to ensure everyone had a gift to open at the party.

That evening dad said we would send my letter to Father Christmas. We did this by me placing my paw on the letter and making a wish. Then dad opened the fire and put it inside, and whoosh, off it went up to Father Christmas. It was so exciting; I hoped so much that it would reach Father Christmas. I only asked for one present as I didn't want to be greedy and living in a small space; I couldn't have too many things.

The next morning, mum shouted to me quite early. We only had two days to go until the Christmas party, and she said I have a big surprise for you, I was very excited and started jumping up and down. She said Vinnie was coming to the party too, and he was bringing his big brother Callum. This was fantastic news. Vinnie was my most favourite little friend ever. His mummy was a special friend of my mum's, so I knew she was happy too. I could introduce them to all my animal friends and my other two special humans, Lily and Noah.

I ran over to see Nyx and told him the good news. We went for a play in the field and chatted about the party. Nyx said she was very excited.

The day before the party arrived, we had to finish preparing the food and make sure all the decorations were in place, and the music was sorted for the games.

Some of the ducks had started to arrive late in the afternoon. They said that they had been too excited to wait until tomorrow. Nyx and I showed them the pond we had made in the big tent for them to play in. They all loved it and said they would take turns so everyone could play and have fun.

We left the ducks as they waddled off to the big pond in the field for the night. Mum said I was to have an early night. Otherwise, I would be too tired tomorrow, so I had my tea and then my treat at seven o'clock like I did every night, and then dad tucked me up under the dinette where my cosy bed is kept.

Today was the day that I had been waiting for what seemed like months. It was nearly eleven o'clock, and my friends had started to arrive; the first one here was Goosy Lucy. She said she had slept on the towpath last night in Braunston, not far away, because she was so excited and wanted to be first here. By half past one, nearly everyone had arrived. I was introducing everyone to each other it was so exciting. Nyx and Digby were running around like mad they loved it.

Suddenly, I saw the cars I had been waiting for; the first was my mum's parents. They had bought Canna, Charlie Clare and Vinnie. Vinnie squealed and got very excited when he saw us all. I gave him a big soppy lick. Then in the other car were Lily, Noah, Primrose, Dale and Dixie with their mum and dad, Gary and Nicky. Wow, today was really amazing.

Everyone quickly went into the big tent, Wayne put some Christmas music on, and we all started dancing. It began to get quite warm in there, and after about five songs, Mum and Amanda decided it was time for us all to have a sit-down and something to eat, so they got the food ready for us.

We had some lovely, tasty food and some delicious drinks too. We were told that after our food we would play games and then there would be a big surprise.

The first game we played was statues, as the grown-ups thought this was best as we better not run about too much after eating all the food. Nyx and Digby struggled and were out very quickly as they couldn't keep still; they were so excited and enjoying the party. Larry llama was the winner and had a lovely prize, a big bag of hay. The next game was in the pond just for all the ducks, geese, moorhens and herons. They had a game of in and out of the hoops. The moorhen won this he was

delighted and made much noise, making me start running around and getting excited. The noise that moorhens make makes me want to chase them, but I know I have to be good and not do that.
We finished the games by having a game of rounders so that all of us could join in; this was for all the humans and animals. The dogs and Llamas were very quick, but marmite the cat just sauntered around at his own speed.

My dad shouted to all the children and animals to go into the big tent because there was going to be a surprise in ten minutes. I called Canna to hurry up as she was swimming in the pond. She loves the water. We all started to chat and ask what each other thought would happen. Noah said he thought we were going to sing songs; Lilly said I don’t think, so I think it's going to be something very, very special.

Then all of a sudden, we heard bells, and then someone shouted HO HO HO, Vinnie jumped and started saying I know who makes that noise, I said I think I know too. Then suddenly, a very tall man dressed in red with a big black belt and a huge bushy beard. Father Christmas had come to our party. WOW, aren't we lucky?

We all sat down, and Father Christmas handed out gifts to everyone. We were told we could open these as it was the Christmas party.
Before father Christmas left, we sang Merry Christmas and thanked him.

We danced and ran around for the next hour while the grownups chatted; it was so much fun having all my friends at the party.

At eight o'clock, mum and dad said it was time to say goodbye to many friends as they had a long way to go home.
I hate saying goodbye, but I know that I will see everyone again, hopefully in not so long.
The good news was that Nyx, Digby, Max, and marmite were all staying at the marina of dreams, too, so we could play lots and lots.

I woke up late the following day. I had lots of lovely dreams about the party and Father Christmas. Mum said that after breakfast, we were all meeting up with Wayne, Amanda, Matt and Claire, plus the dogs and tidying up the mess. I didn't really want to tidy up but was pleased to see my friends. I quickly went to chat with them and asked what they had thought of the party. They loved seeing all the other animals, but their favourite was when Father Christmas came in.
We only had one more sleep before Father Christmas came to our boats. We all started to ask how he would get in and what we thought we might have for Christmas. I said that I would like a new ball and a chewy stick. Mum said we would all have to wait and

see in the morning as Father Christmas had a magic key and could always get into people's houses.

At last, it was Christmas eve. I had my tea and put out some biscuits, a glass of milk for Father Christmas, and a couple of carrots for the reindeer.

I woke up early and jumped at mum and dad's bedroom door. I was so excited. Mum and dad came through into the lounge area of the boat, and guess what? Father Christmas had eaten his biscuits, drank his milk, and even the carrots had gone. WOW, how wonderful. Then on the settee, I spotted a bag mum said was for me, with lots of presents. I was so happy and very grateful for my gifts. Dad got dressed and took me outside. Nyx came running over to me. He was so very excited and bouncing up and down. He told me Father Christmas had crept into the boat and left him some presents too. We went for a run-around, and Digby, Max, and Marmite came to see us too, and guess what? Father Christmas had visited their boat too.

When we all returned to our boats, mum called Lily and Noah to wish them a happy Christmas. They were all very excited, and guess what? Yes, Father Christmas had visited their boat too. He had been very busy last night, I thought. I bet he was very tired. The last phone call was to Claire's house to wish Vinnie a happy Christmas, Father Christmas had even sneaked into their house, and Vinnie had lots of presents he was still opening. This had been a wonderful morning. We all had been so lucky; the Christmas dinner was still coming, and I heard I was having one too. Plus, my mum's mum and dad were coming for dinner and bringing canna back, too. Yay, this made me have a big smile.

Christmas is my favourite time of the year, mainly because I see all my favourite animals and my favourite humans, have lots of fun and even get presents.
The afternoon was finished with all the animals popping to the marina to see us, and I gave them all a present, so they didn't miss out. Mum said it is nice to give gifts too.

Draw your picture of your Christmas morning, and email it to mexiboatdog@gmail.com
Or you can write your own story and send that too.

Draw your picture of your Christmas morning, and email it to mexiboatdog@gmail.com
Or you can write your own story and send that too.

Draw your picture of your Christmas morning, and email it to mexiboatdog@gmail.com
Or you can write your own story and send that too.

Printed in Great Britain
by Amazon